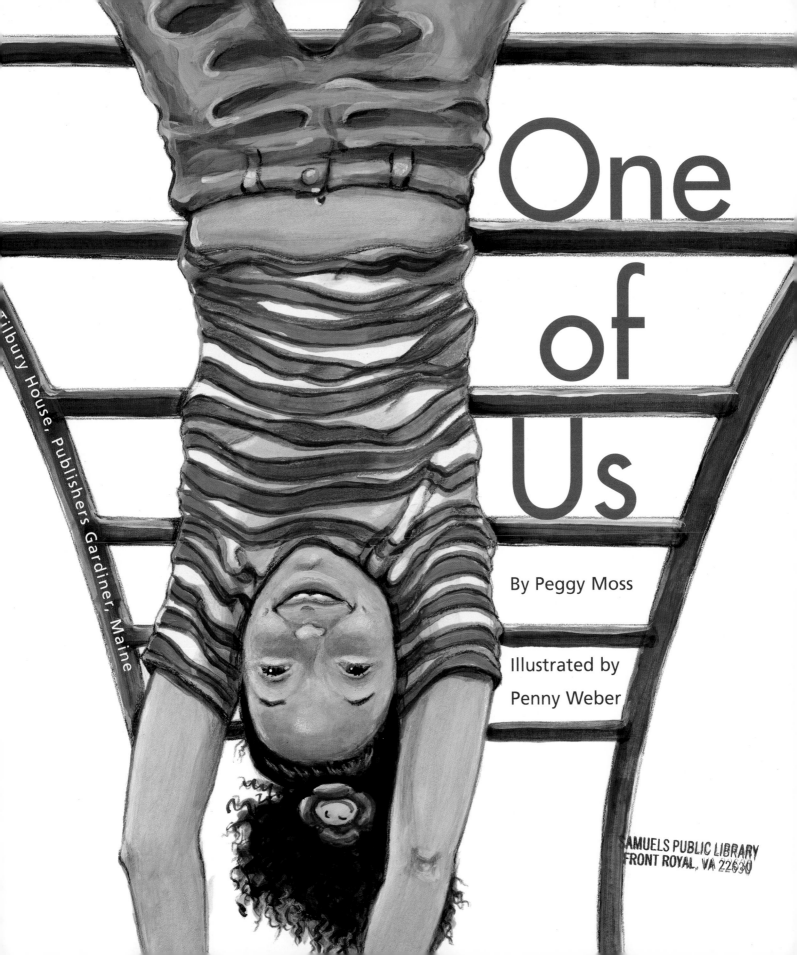

One
of
Us

By Peggy Moss

Illustrated by
Penny Weber

Tilbury House, Publishers Gardiner, Maine

Roberta James put her hair up. Straight up. And walked into Baker School.

She was late. Two weeks late.

"We just moved here," Roberta explained to the principal.

"Welcome to Baker School," the principal said. "I think you are going to love it here."

The principal was right. Roberta loved the brightly painted walls and the library full of books. She thought the playground looked fabulous.

When Roberta got to her classroom, she met Carmen.

"Sit here," Carmen said.

"You are one of us."

Roberta sat.

At recess, Roberta ran
toward the monkey bars.

"We don't play on the
playground," Carmen said.
"We sit here and talk."

Roberta smiled, "Thank you, but
actually, I love the monkey bars."
She met Rodney there, and
Jasmine and Katie.

"You're one of us!" Jasmine said.
"Sit with us at lunch."

At lunchtime, Roberta picked up her daisy lunchbox and walked over to the Monkey Bar Gang. They all had monkey lunchboxes. "Kids with flowers on their lunchboxes sit over there," Katie said. She scrunched up her face and pointed.

"I wish I had a flowered lunchbox," Rodney said.

"That's ridiculous," Katie said. "You're a boy."

Roberta looked at the flowered-lunchbox kids. They waved.

"You're one of us!" Emiko said.

"Come on over!" Emily called.

Roberta walked over. She was feeling a little confused as she sat down. "What's in there?" Emiko asked.

Roberta took out her mother's famous mayonnaise and coconut pita roll-up with raisins stuffed into the ends. Everyone at the table stared.

"Kids who eat that kind of stuff sit over there," Emiko said.

Roberta looked across the lunchroom.
A group of kids eating pita roll-ups waved.

"Come on over," one of them said.

"You're one of us," another shouted.
They were all wearing cowboy boots.

"Who are you?" Anna asked.

"Roberta James," Roberta said.

"I mean—what are you?" Anna said.

"I am a straight-up-hair girl who climbs monkey bars and carries a flowered lunchbox with a pita roll-up in it. And I wear running shoes," Roberta said.

"Oh—," Anna said, very slowly. "So you're one of US."

"I doubt it," Roberta said. "What are you?"

"I am a trumpet-playing girl who likes baseball and car racing and ballet," Anna said.

"I love building things and spicy food and origami and bowling," Jason said.

"I like spicy food," Roberta said. "I love baseball, but I'm not crazy about ballet."

"Perfect," Jason said.

"But we aren't the same," Roberta said.

"That's the best part," Anna said.

"How was your first day?" The principal asked as Roberta got ready to go home.

"Pretty good," Roberta said.

"I bet you fit right in," the principal said.

Roberta giggled. "Yeah, I guess I do."

TILBURY HOUSE, PUBLISHERS
103 Brunswick Avenue, Gardiner, Maine 04345
800–582–1899 · www.tilburyhouse.com

First hardcover edition: June 2010 · 10 9 8 7 6 5 4 3 2 1

For Ted and Paula Moss—and for you. Be as you are. —PM

For Gerard, Thank you! —PW

Library of Congress Cataloging-in-Publication Data
Moss, Peggy, 1966-
  One of us / Peggy Moss ; illustrated by Penny Weber. —
1st hardcover ed.
       p. cm.
  Summary: Roberta is welcomed by different
groups on her first day at a new school, only
to be told she does not fit in with them for some
reason, but by the next day, members of each
group have begun to see that they do not have
to be alike in every way.
  ISBN 978-0-88448-322-9 (hardcover : alk. paper)
[1. Individuality—Fiction. 2. Friendship—Fiction.
3. Schools—Fiction. 4. Moving, Household—
Fiction.] I. Weber, Penny, ill. II. Title.
  PZ7.M85357One 2010
  [E]—dc22
                        2009046325

Designed by Geraldine Millham, Westport, Massachusetts.
Printed and bound by Sung In Printing Ltd., Dang Jung-Dong 242-2,
GungPo-si, Kyunggi-do, Korea; February 2010.